D0961601

© 1993 Geddes & Grosset Ltd
Reprinted 1994
Published by Geddes & Grosset Ltd,
New Lanark, Scotland.

ISBN  1 85534 565 X

Printed and bound in Slovenia.

# The Hare and The Tortoise

Retold by Judy Hamilton
Illustrated by Lyndsay Duff

**Tarantula Books**

It was a lovely sunny day, but the animals in the forest were paying no attention to the weather. They were arguing about which of them could run the fastest. Hare, as usual, was boasting.

"I am the fastest by far! I will race any one of you. The prize will be this gold button. Squirrel, how about you?"

"No fear, Hare, not I," giggled Squirrel "your legs are too long for me!"

"Fox, do you want to race me?"

Fox shook his head silently.

"Is nobody brave enough to try to beat me in a race? Badger? Hedgehog? Weasel? ...... Nobody?"

There was silence for a moment or two, and then a tiny voice said, "I'll have a try, if you like!"

Hare turned round to see where the voice was coming from and saw Tortoise plodding slowly across the field at the edge of the forest.

Hare giggled quietly to himself but tried to keep his face straight as he spoke to Tortoise.

"Ah. Tortoise my good fellow! So you have joined us—at last!"

"I saw no reason to hurry, " said Tortoise. "It's such a lovely day, after all."

Hare held the button up in front of him so that it sparkled in the sunshine.

"It seems, Tortoise, that you are my only challenger. Are you willing, then, to race me to the stone bridge on the other side of the wood? This is a fine prize, you must admit!"

"Very fine prize, Hare; it certainly is a very fine prize. And a race to the bridge across the woods sounds fair enough to me. Yes, Hare, I am willing to race you," Tortoise spoke slowly and carefully.

Hare burst out laughing.

"Old Slowcoach, you can't be serious! You have no chance of beating me in a race! You *must* be joking!"

The other animals joined in the laughter.

Tortoise shook his head slowly. "Indeed I am not joking!" he assured them all. "Now, who is going to start us off?"

Hare was still laughing as the two animals lined up and waited for Owl's starting signal.

"Tu-whit tu-whoo!"

The "tu-whoo" had hardly left Owl's beak when the hare was off like the wind, speeding through the trees. The tortoise was still plodding into the edge of the woods when the hare was already out of sight.

"Come on Tortoise!" cheered the other animals laughingly. "Can't you go any faster than that?"

"I don't know why you bother, Tortoise!" said Badger. "Anyone can see that Hare will win by miles!"

Tortoise didn't like these unkind remarks very much at all, but he did not show that his feelings were hurt. Instead, he just kept plodding on, all the time saying to himself;

"Slow and steady wins the race, slow and steady......"

Hare charged on relentlessly through the woods, hopping over a tree stump here and there, weaving in and out of the clumps of bracken. After a while he paused for a moment and listened. There was no sound of anything following him. He turned round and looked back through the trees. There was no sign of Tortoise. The hare chuckled to himself. He was winning by miles. He lolloped on at a more gentle pace for a few more minutes and then stopped again. He was now at the far edge of the wood, and a short distance in front of him he could see the old stone bridge, the finishing post of the race.

But there were no other animals there to watch Hare in his moment of glory as he reached the finish. Hare, being a bit of a show-off, didn't like the idea of finishing without anyone there to cheer him. So he decided to wait for a little while, until some of the other animals caught up with him. He settled himself down under a tree to wait. Once a crowd had gathered, he thought, he would make a triumphant dash for the bridge and for victory.

But it was a hot day, and Hare had to close his eyes against the glare of the sun. And it was a very comfortable place to rest . . . . .

In the twinkling of an eye, Hare dozed off to sleep.

It was very late in the afternoon when Hare woke up again. The sun was no longer fierce and hot. It was beginning to sink down behind the trees. Across his whiskers Hare could feel the beginnings of a cool evening breeze. As he got up, he caught the sounds of other creatures in a state of excitement—sniffling, twittering, squeaking and hooting.

"Goody! They're here to see me win the race!" he thought.

"Poor old Tortoise. I bet he's miles behind!"

Hare had a little stretch, and got ready to run again.

Hare did not know, however, that all the time that he had been sleeping contentedly in the sunshine, the tortoise had been trudging slowly but steadily on through the woods.

And Hare had been asleep for a very long time— long enough, in fact, for Tortoise to catch up with him, and slowly but steadily to pass him. Hare did not know that the animals were cheering Tortoise and not him. Hare did not know that Tortoise was now only a couple of steps away from the old stone bridge . . .

All of a sudden, Hare caught sight of Tortoise. With horror, he realized what had happened.

He could not believe how silly he had been. But there it was for all to see. It did not matter how hard he ran now, for it was too late to catch up with Tortoise! All the other animals were there to see Tortoise win the race!

The gentle, sensible tortoise plodded the last two steps to the stone bridge with a smile on his face. He had won. He was very, very hot and tired, but he didn't care one bit about that. He had beaten the show-off Hare! The other animals cheered and cheered.

"Good old Tortoise! Well done! You're the winner!"

The noise was music to Tortoise's ears as he huffed and puffed and panted.

Putting his tiredness to one side for a moment, the Tortoise took a few more brave steps up to the top of the bridge and stood there, glowing with pride and waving shyly to the cheering crowd. It was one of the happiest moments in his life.

Poor, foolish Hare! How embarrassed he was to think of everybody watching him sleeping as Tortoise passed him by!

How ashamed he was that he had let himself be beaten by a tortoise! How sorry he was that he had been so big-headed and boastful!

"Here you are, Tortoise. Here's the golden button prize," he muttered, ears drooping. "And—well done!"

The other animals were laughing fit to burst.

"Its all right, Hare," said Tortoise kindly, "you can keep the button. "I've had a lot of fun today. But in future, just remember; slow and steady wins the race, slow and steady . . ."